Farmer Donald's Pumpkin Patch

By Susan Ring

Illustrated by Loter, Inc.

Disney PRESS

New York

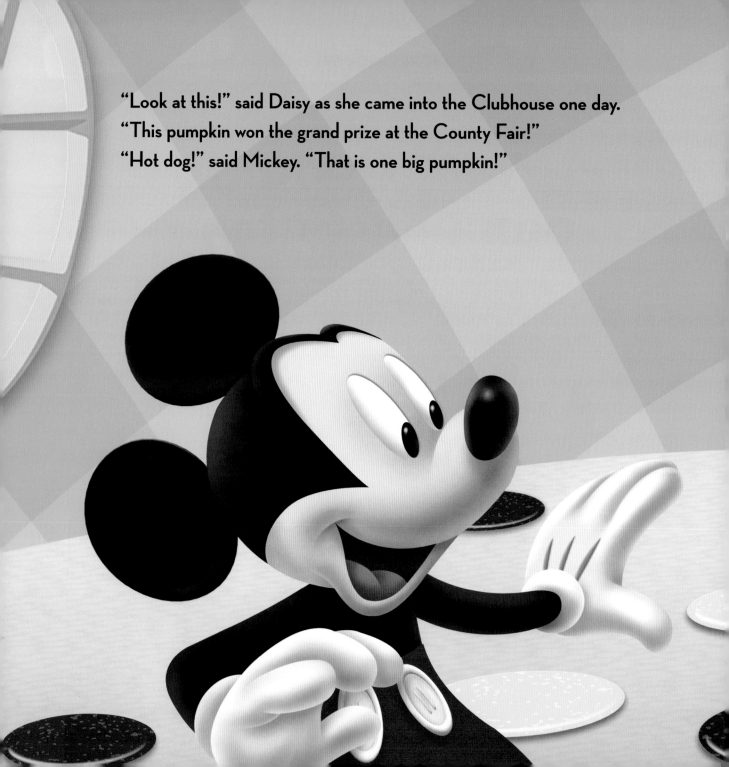

"Look at this!" said Daisy as she came into the Clubhouse one day.
"This pumpkin won the grand prize at the County Fair!"
"Hot dog!" said Mickey. "That is one big pumpkin!"

Donald took a look at the picture. "Aw, phooey!" he said. "I could grow a garden filled with the biggest pumpkins you've ever seen!" Donald declared. "I'm sure it's easy to do."

The next day, Donald got pumpkin seeds and threw them on the dirt.
"I think it takes more than that to grow a garden," said Minnie.
Mickey nodded. "First you need to make holes in the dirt, put a seed
in each hole, and then cover them up."

"That's a lot of work," said Donald.

"Maybe Toodles can help," said Mickey. "Oh, Toodles!"

Toodles showed them a pogo stick, a mirror, and an elephant.
"Hmm," Donald said. "Which Mouseketool can help us make holes for the seeds?"
"I think it's this one," said Minnie, as she pointed to the pogo stick.

Minnie was right! The pogo stick made holes that were just the right size. Then Donald dropped a seed into each hole and covered them all with dirt.

"See, I told you this would be easy," said Donald as he sat back down. "Now all we have to do is watch the seeds grow."

Donald, thinking his work was done, closed his eyes to rest.
"I think it takes more than that to grow a garden," said Daisy.
"A garden needs water," Mickey said. "Water helps seeds grow."

"Mickey's right," said Minnie.
"But how am I going to water this big garden?" asked Donald.
"That's a lot of work."

"It's time to call Toodles again," said Mickey. "Oh, Toodles!"

"Let's pick the elephant," said Daisy, looking at the remaining tools.
Daisy was right! First the elephant took a big drink from the pond.
Then, using her trunk, she sprinkled water over the entire garden.

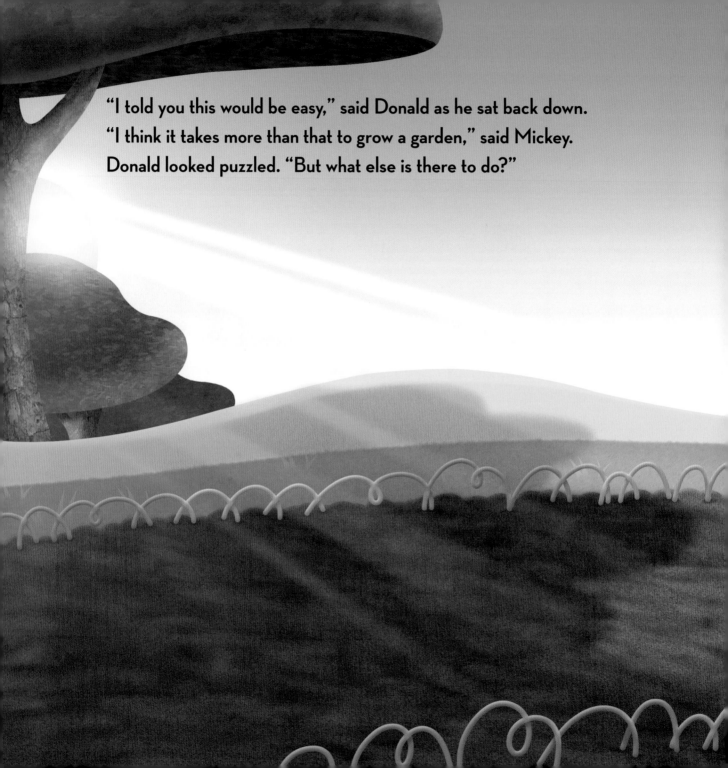

"I told you this would be easy," said Donald as he sat back down.
"I think it takes more than that to grow a garden," said Mickey.
Donald looked puzzled. "But what else is there to do?"

"Plants need sun," said Minnie. "But your garden is in the shade."

"But we can't move the sun!" exclaimed Donald.

"Maybe we can," said Mickey. "Oh, Toodles!"

Toodles had just one tool left—a mirror.
"A mirror?" asked Donald. "How can that help my garden grow?"
Mickey and Minnie placed the mirror so that it reflected the sunlight onto the garden.

"Oh, boy!" shouted Donald. "Now we'll just watch the seeds grow."
Daisy giggled. "*Now* we have to make sure the garden keeps getting
plenty of water and sunlight and care, Farmer Donald!"

Donald discovered that growing a garden wasn't as easy as he expected. But over the next few months, he worked hard. When it was time for the pumpkin contest, Donald picked the biggest, most beautiful pumpkin from his garden, and then the whole gang headed to the fair.

Judge Goofy walked around and looked at all the pumpkins. Finally he said, "The prize for the biggest pumpkin goes to Farmer Donald!"
"Next year, I think I'll enter the apple-pie contest," said Daisy.
"Good idea!" Donald declared. "I'll plant a great big apple orchard so you'll have all the apples you need. I'm sure it's easy to do."